Let's right the wrong.

Keep going— never stop.

STAY STRONG.

Follow your heart.

BE BRAVE.

THANK YOU.

Let's stand together.

LISTEN and LEARN.

LET'S MAKE OUR WORLD A MORE COLORFUL PLACE.

HATE HAS NO HOME HERE.

Be the change you want to see happen.

PEACE.

Together is BETTER.

TURN ENERGY INTO ACTION.

We've only just begun.

GOOD KARMA BEGETS GOOD KARMA.

To Emma González
and all people who are brave enough to
say something—and move the world to a better
place—inspiring others to do the same. —P.H.R.

All rights reserved. Published by Orchard Books, an imprint of Scholastic Inc., *Publishers since 1920.* ORCHARD BOOKS and design are registered trademarks of Watts Publishing Group, Ltd., used under license. SCHOLASTIC and associated logos are trademarks and/or registered trademarks of Scholastic Inc.
Library of Congress Cataloging-in-Publication Data available
ISBN 978-0-545-86503-6
10 9 8 7 6 5 4 3 2 1   19 20 21 22 23
Printed in China   62 • First edition, March 2019
The text type and display are hand-lettered by Peter H. Reynolds.
Reynolds Studio assistance by Julia Anne Young • Book design by Patti Ann Harris

SAY
SOMETHING!

by PETER HAMILTON REYNOLDS

ORCHARD BOOKS
AN IMPRINT of SCHOLASTIC INC.

You don't have to be loud.

Powerful words can be a whisper.

You can say something in **so many ways.**

With words, with action, with creativity.

If you see
someone lonely...

SAY SOMETHING by planting a seed and watching it bloom.

If you see someone
being hurt...

If you see something **beautiful**...

SAY SOMETHING
to help people understand.

Sometimes you'll say something
and no one will be listening.

But keep saying
what is in your heart...

... and you will find
someone
who listens.

Keep saying it...

...and you may be surprised
to find the whole world
listening.

Some people find it easier to SAY SOMETHING than others...

I hope...

I believe...

I wish...

I'm ready to change the world.

Join US!

Together, we can...

I imagine...

...but everyone has something to say.

Your voice can
inspire, heal, and transform.
Your voice can change the world.

Are you ready
to say something?

PETER HAMILTON REYNOLDS